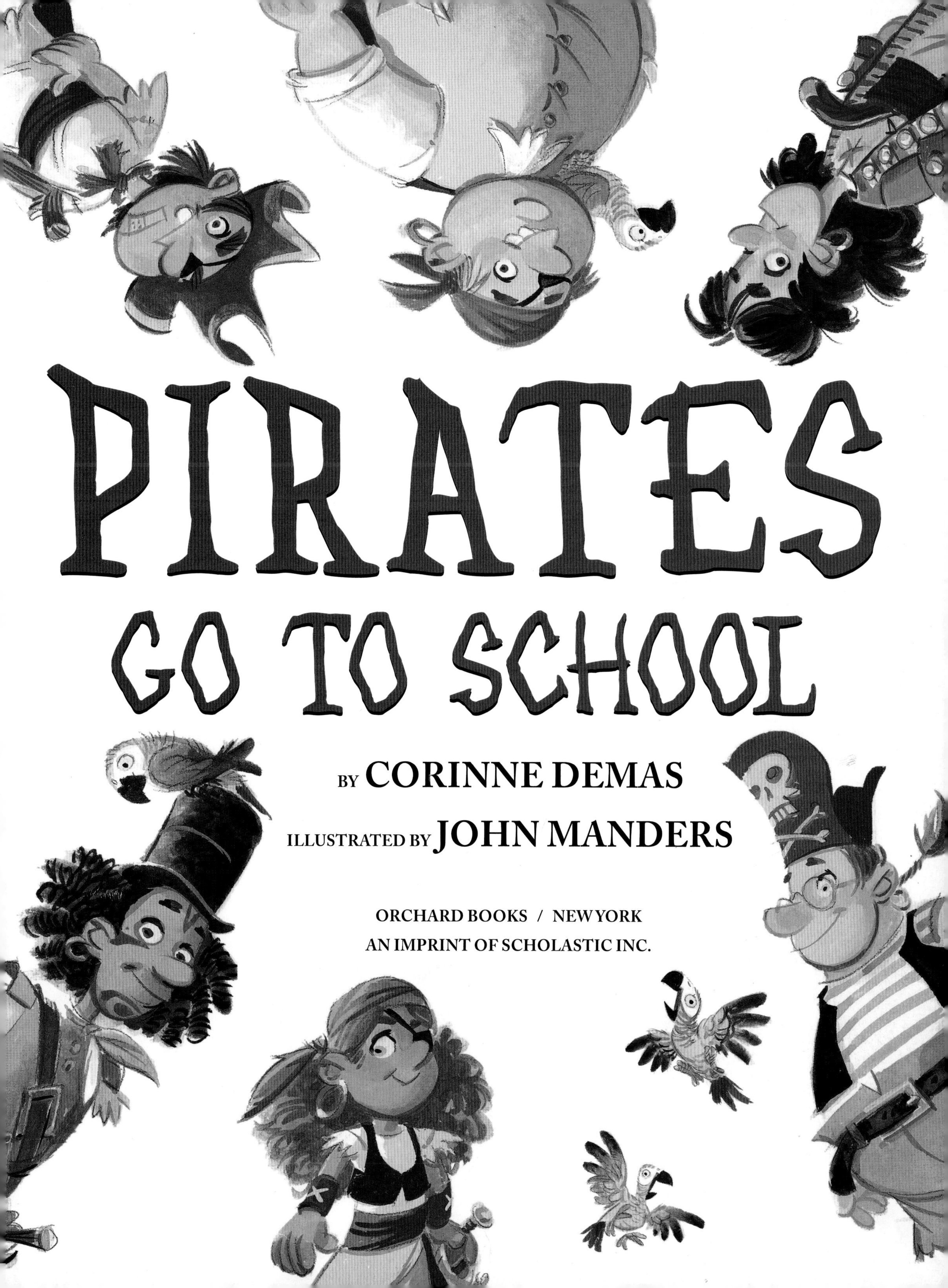

PIRATES GO TO SCHOOL

BY CORINNE DEMAS

ILLUSTRATED BY JOHN MANDERS

ORCHARD BOOKS / NEW YORK
AN IMPRINT OF SCHOLASTIC INC.

Library of Congress Cataloging-in-Publication Data

Demas, Corinne.

Pirates go to school / by Corinne Demas ; illustrated by John Manders. — 1st ed. p. cm.

Summary: A rhyming tale of pirates who go to school accompanied by their parrots, learn arithmetic and letters, and want to hear sea stories at story time.

ISBN 978-0-545-20629-7 (alk. paper)

[1. Stories in rhyme. 2. Pirates—Fiction. 3. Schools—Fiction.] I. Manders, John, ill.

II. Title. PZ8.3.D3888Pi 2011 [E]—dc22 2010031394

10 9 8 7 6 5 15

First edition, July 2011

Printed in Malaysia 108

The artwork was created using watercolors, gouache, and colored pencil.

The text was set in Adobe Casalon Pro Semibold.

The display type was set in Flyerfonts WhiteHouse.

Book design by Marijka Kostiw

FOR OUR CUTE LITTLE PIRATES:

MORGAN, CLAY, CYRUS, GARIN,

AND TEGAN – C.D.

TO THE MEMORY OF SHERMAN,

THE BEST PARROT A PIRATE

COULD WISH FOR – J.M.

Pirates come to school each day
with backpacks full of books.
They hang their pirate swords up
on the coatrack on the hooks.

Pirates bring their parrots,

who echo what they say:

"Good morning, Teacher!"

"Good morning, Teacher!"

is how they start each day.

To sit next to a pirate

is everybody's wish,

but better hold your nose because

they smell of rotting fish.

Pirates learn their letters:

X (marks the spot), Y, Z.

Pirates learn arithmetic:

Two skulls plus one is three.

AaBbCcDdEeFfGgHh
1+2 =

Pirates like to paint black skies,

make cannonballs with clay.

Pirates bring home artwork

to their pirate ship each day.

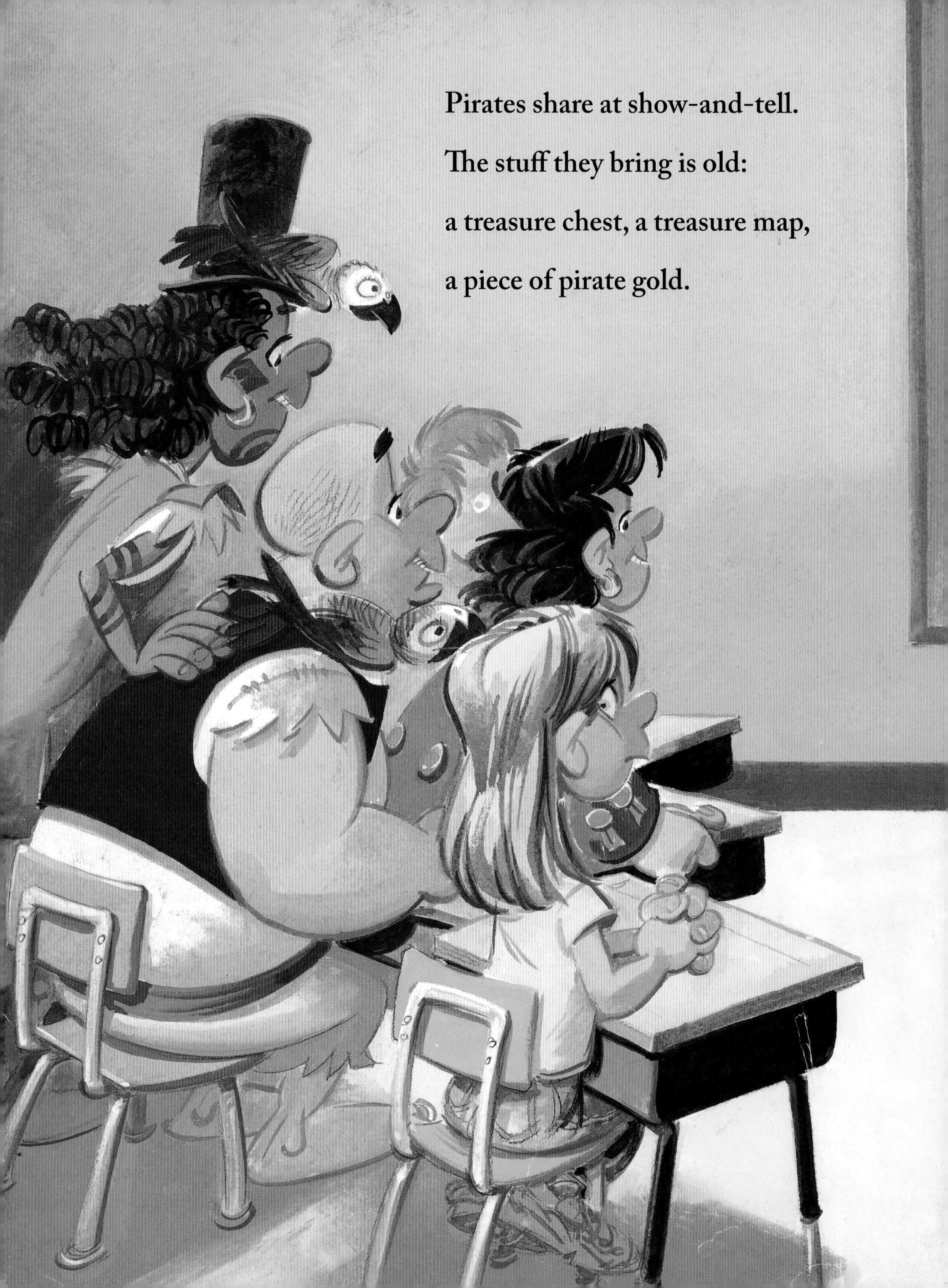

Pirates share at show-and-tell.

The stuff they bring is old:

a treasure chest, a treasure map,

a piece of pirate gold.

Pirates won't eat peanut butter;

they won't touch cheese or carrots.

At snack time they want slimy squid,

and crackers for their parrots.

Pirates nap at nap time,

since that's what nap time's for.

The only trouble is . . .

pirates always snore!

Pirates play at "walk the plank"

and other games quite daring.

But then the teacher calls time-out

because she hears them swearing.

"We hate time-outs! (Aargh!)"

"We hate time-outs! (Aargh!)"

pirates and parrots roar.

"Behave yourselves," the teacher warns,

"or you'll sit five minutes more."

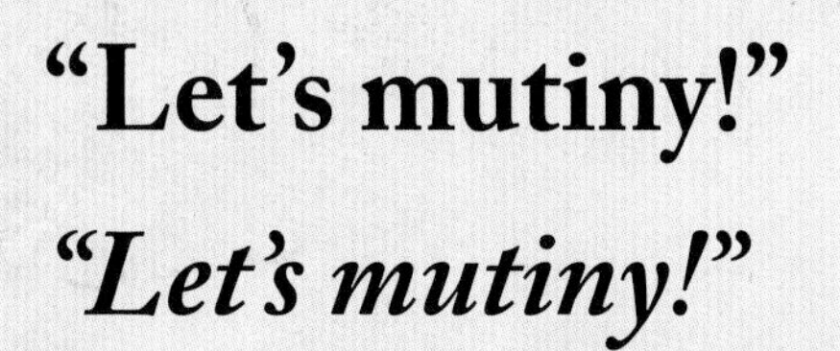

"Let's mutiny!"

"Let's mutiny!"

pirates and parrots cry.

But wait! It's almost story time,

so pirates do not try.

At story time the pirates beg
for tales of ships at sea,
and at the end they spin some yarns
of pirate treachery.

OoPpQqRrSsTtUuVvWwXxYyZz

When the school day's over,

pirates put everything away.

They clean the mess their parrots made

and this is what they say:

"Yo ho ho,
we're so cool.
We are pirates
and we love school."